Jack's road

Rigby®

A Harcourt Achieve Imprint

www.Rigby.com
1-800-531-5015

"Look at my road,"

said Jack.

3

"My car is on the road,"

said Jack.

"Look at my bus,"

said Billy.

"Look at my **bus!**"

said Billy.

"Can my bus go

on the road?" said Billy.

"My car is on the road,"

said Jack.

"My truck is on the road,"

said Jack.

"My **bus** is on the road,"

said Billy.